Tía María's Garden

Tía
María's Garden

by Ann Nolan Clark

Illustrated by Ezra Jack Keats

New York · The Viking Press

To Mary and Jonathan

6

Tía María's garden
has no fences.
It goes on and on
from our door
to where the sky
bends down
to touch the land.

Tía María
    does not like fences.
They keep things in,
    too much.
They keep things out,
    too much.
We do not like fences,
    Tía María and I.

In Tía María's garden
    there is desert sand.
Sun likes the sand,
    I think, because
    even in the morning
    he touches it
    to make it warm.

Wind likes the desert, too.
All day long
    he runs along the sand,
    playing with it.
He tosses it here and there
    and winds it up
    into spinning whirlwinds.

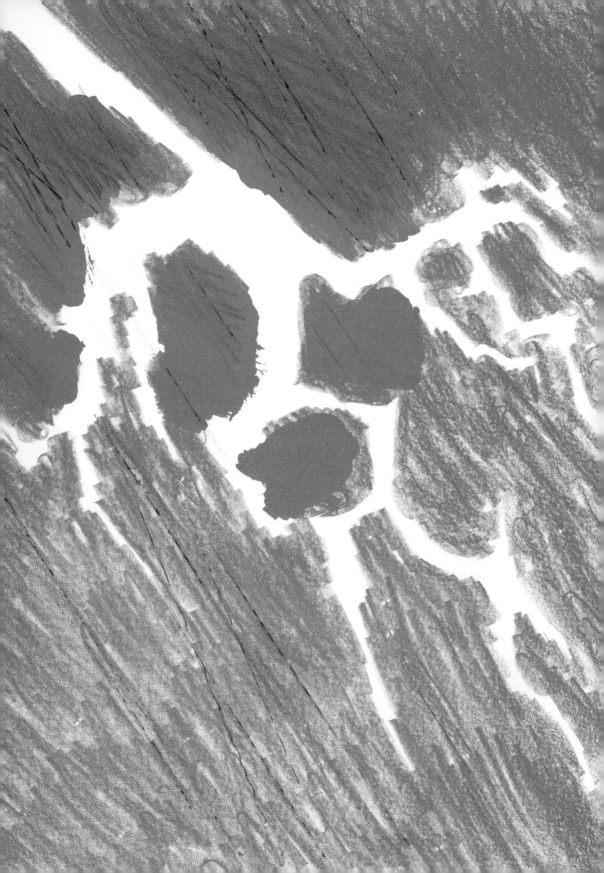

Rain is too busy
    to come often
    to Tía María's garden.
When he does come
    he brings thunder and lightning
    and floods everything
    so we won't forget him.

In Tía María's garden
    the grass bunches
    and cactus and bushes
    are there because
    they want to be.
We do not need
    to plant them.

12   We walk a long way
        and look at everything.
     We see tracks
        in the sand,
        footprints of wild things
        leaving their marks
        so we can know them.

Every morning
    when Sun comes up,
    Tía María and I walk
    in her garden.
Wind and Sand walk
    with us,
    wanting to be friends.

14

We walk along, walk along,
    not talking, just looking.
I see Something!
I see Jack Rabbit,
    sand-colored Jack Rabbit
    with black braid on his coat
    and white mittens on his ears.

I see him. I see him.
He is eating the cactus.
He sees me, too, and

with a hop and a jump
he leaps over the cactus,
and wigwags good-by
with his button white tail.

Away off somewhere
     we hear the bell song
     of the desert dove.
Here where we walk
     there is only stillness.
The desert is so still
     I can almost hear it.

I see the tracks
    of Desert Sidewinder.
Desert Sidewinder is bad,
    that's what they say,
    but he makes pretty marks
    on the sand where he crawls,
    like the fingerpainting
    I make with my hands.

Desert Sidewinder,
    if you are nearby
    and can see me
    or hear me,
    please know that I know
    you don't want
    to be bad.

We walk along,
   walk along,
   and Wind walks
   with us.

We walk along,
   walk along,
   and a long thin lizard
   with a long thin tail
   runs in front
   of me,
   stops to look back
   at me,
   does push-ups
   for me,
   one-two-three-four,
   one-two-three-four,
   just to show
   he is not afraid.

We come
    to a waterhole
    that Rain left
    for the wild things
    to have water
    to drink.

We sit in the shade
    of a giant cactus
    and watch quail come
    to the waterhole.

They are wearing red hats
    and Sunday dresses
    like ladies going to church,
    taking their children
    with them
    and making them use
    their going-to-church manners.

Above us
Woodpecker pecks
the spiny ribs
of the giant cactus
making a nest-hole.
Elf Owl watches,
planning to move in
when Woodpecker finishes
pecking the nest-hole.

I see a little horny toad,
    a flat, fat, spiny horny toad.
I pick him up
    to say hello.
He looks as if
    he wants to know
    about my house
    and how I live,
    and so
    I put him in my pocket.

Tía María's garden
has all kinds
of cactus,
giant, prickly pear,
pincushion, and cholla.
I count them on my fingers
but not on my thumb,
giant, prickly pear,
pincushion, and cholla.

Giant Cactus
    has twisted arms
    that reach, almost,
    to the sky.
Giant Cactus goes marching
    up all the hillsides
    but never marches down again.
Woodpecker and Elf Owl
    make their homes
    in the giant cactus.
Its spines do not hurt them.

Prickly Pear has paddles
    full of sharp spines.
Jack Rabbit eats them,
    spines and paddles.
I think he likes them.
Trade Rat makes her nest
    under them
    to keep her babies safe.

Pincushion Cactus
    looks like the pineapple
    Tía María gave me
    for my breakfast,
    but the pineapple
    does not prick me
    when I touch it.
You do, Pincushion Cactus.
Do you want to prick me?

Cholla Cactus
    hides in the arroyo
    and shows its branches
    over the arroyo bank.
They look like
    the spreading antlers
    of a deer.

Morning Sun
    is shining brighter.
Morning Shadows
    are getting shorter.
We have rested
    by the cactus.
Now is time
    to go home again.

We turned homeward,
    walking slowly
    across the sand.
I have a feeling
    that the wild things
    and the wild plants
    do not want us
    to go away.

Tía María's garden
    is so full of
    so many things.
Having just
    two feet
    and two eyes
    and two ears
    does not let me
    go far enough,
    or see enough,
    or hear enough,
    to make me know
    all I want to know
    in Tía María's garden.

The sand
    gets in my sandals.
It is heavy
    on my feet.
The wind
    pushes against me.
It makes my walking
    a little slow.
But I am glad, Tía María,
    that we came
    this way
    this morning.
We have seen
    so many things.

Now we come
to the place
I like best
of all.

In the sand
standing still
is a river of rock
that has no water
in its rocky bed.
Tía María calls it
a rocky rise
in the desert floor
but I call it
my river of rock.

My river of rock
    has no water,
    just has rocks,
    broken rocks
    of different sizes
    and different shapes.
It just has rocks,
    colored rocks
    that Sunset painted
    with marks
    and stripes
    and crooked lines.

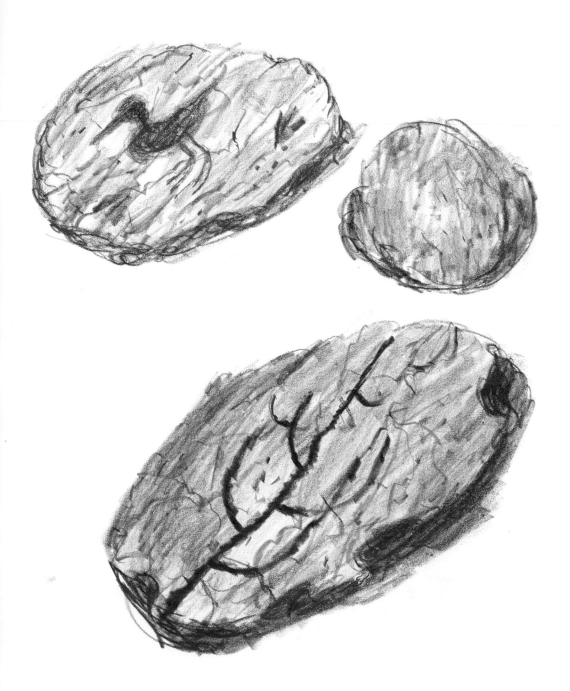

I found a rock
      as big as my hand.
It had a duck
      painted on it.
I found another one,
      a green one
      with a painted
      black tree.

I stay a long time,
      filling my pockets
      with pieces of rock.
Each new one
      is prettier
      than the last one
      I found.

Tía María says
    that we must go.
She says the rocks
    will be here
    tomorrow.

So we start walking,
    but my pockets
    are too heavy.
They are heavier
    than I am.

After a while
    we get to our house.
It is a good house.
Its door is always open.

By the door
    is a bird feeder
    with Saint Francis
    saying to the birds,
    "Come and eat."

By the door
    is a wall
    where the quail come
    to rest and to drink
    at the pool.

We sit by the pool
    where the goldfish swim.
We drink lemonade
    that is wet and cool.

Tomorrow we will walk again
   in Tía María's garden.
Tomorrow, tomorrow,
   who knows about tomorrow?
Tomorrow we may reach the place
   where the sky bends down
   to touch the land.

E
CLA   Clark, Ann Nolan

         Tia Maria's garden

E
CLA   Clark, Ann Nolan

         Tia Maria's garden

1972

DATE	BORROWER'S NAME	
JAN 23	Theresa Mendez 20	
	K. Twotog	
DEC 19		
APR 25	Dale 18	
MAR 4	Janet B	
MAY 21	Lisa	